The Baby Clause 2.0

MELANIE MORELAND

Edited by:
Jeanne McDonald

Interior design & formatting by:
Christine Borgford, Type A Formatting

Cover design by:
Melissa Ringuette, Monark Design Services

This is for you.

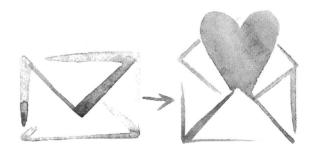

Because you loved the book so much and asked for more.

Chapter 1

TURNING INTO THE large entrance of the hospital, I slammed on the brakes so hard my car shuddered. My tires squealed and left black marks on the pavement. Flinging open the door, I lunged out of the seat, not even bothering to shut the door behind me. I was lucky I remembered to take the keys.

A security guard stopped me before I made it to the sliding doors of the hospital, holding up his hand.

"Sir, you can't leave your car there. The parking lot is across the street—"

I interrupted him, shaking my head. I tossed my keys in his direction. "Look, kid, I trust you. Park my car and bring me the keys."

"I can't do that!"

Reaching into my pocket, I grabbed a wad of cash. I had no idea how much it was, but to this kid standing in front of me, blocking my way, masking his youth by pretending to be forceful, I was certain it was a fortune. I shoved the money into his hand, smirking as his eyes widened at the sight of the cash.

"Sure you can. Think of it as a reward for a job well done. Park my car and bring me my keys." I pushed past him.

"Where are you going, sir?" he shouted.

I glanced over my shoulder as I hurried away. "The maternity ward!"

I TAPPED MY foot as I waited for the elevator. My heart beat frantically, hands clenching and unclenching at my side, thinking about the call I received while having lunch with a client and Graham.

"Hello?"

"Richard, it's Laura. I need you to come to the hospital."

Ice flooded my veins. "What?"

"Katy's gone into labor."

I was on my feet, rushing out of the restaurant without another thought. I heard my name being called, but I ignored it. I jumped in my car, speeding toward the hospital. Katy wasn't due for another three weeks. The baby was early. I had to get to her immediately.

The doors opened, and I cursed under my breath as I waited for people to exit. Didn't they know I was in a hurry? I pressed six on the panel, then hit the 'door close' button, even though people were still filing in. My head fell back on my shoulders, as I inhaled a deep breath and counted to ten. I endured the slow ascent upward, trying not to snarl at people as they got off on other floors. I pushed the 'door close' button constantly, ignoring the frowns sent my way.

When the door opened on six, I burst out of the elevator, running to the desk. A nurse entering some information into the computer ignored me.

"My wife—"

She held up her hand, stopping me, and continued to type, not at all concerned with my panic. I wanted to scream, but I fisted my hands and held my tongue. Katy constantly told me I needed to learn patience. A few seconds later, she looked up with a bright smile.

"How can I help you?"

"My wife—I got a call—she's having the baby today!"

"And the name?"

I stared at her, my brow furrowed. "We don't *know* the name. The baby hasn't been born yet."

She scowled and opened her mouth, but I kept talking.

"How would I know the name? We didn't want to know the sex. We wanted it to be a surprise. But she's gone into labor early. I got a call. I need to find her."

"Your *wife's* name, sir."

I sucked in a deep breath. Well, *that* made more sense.

"Katharine—but I call her Katy. She likes that better."

She arched an eyebrow.

I said nothing in return, just glared. *What the hell else did she want?*

A hand fell on my shoulder, and I startled, looking down to see the amused face of Dr. Suzanne Simon. She patted my shoulder. "Calm, Richard. Katy is fine." She smiled at the nurse. "VanRyan, Shelly. It's Katy VanRyan."

The nurse named Shelly grinned and threw me a look that made me think she was laughing at me. "I wondered. She warned me."

I looked between the two of them. *Warned? Who warned her? About what exactly?*

Dr. Suzanne squeezed my arm. "Come with me, Richard. I'll take you to Katy, and then I'll explain everything."

I nodded, following her down the hall, my stomach tense and my nerves tight.

"What did she mean, 'she warned me'?"

Suzanne glanced up with a knowing look on her face. "Katy said she had a feeling you'd be a bit less *in control* than usual today. 'Freaked out,' I think were her words."

I opened my mouth to protest, then shut it with a snap. As usual, my wife was right. I *was* rather freaked out right now. I needed to see Katy so I could calm down.

Suzanne stopped in front of a door, regarding me patiently. "Katy is fine. The baby is fine. You need to be composed and strong for her, all right?"

I exhaled hard. "Yes."

"She needs you."

"She's really all right? The baby is early."

"Babies come early all the time, Richard. With all the books you've read and the questions you've asked, you *know* this can happen. Katy is young and healthy. You also know I would never hold anything back from you."

I relaxed a little hearing the honesty in her voice—and she was right. I had read a ton of books, and asked endless questions. Suzanne had always been honest, blunt, and to the point with us. She wouldn't tell me Katy was okay unless she was, indeed, all right.

"Okay. I'm good. Can I see her now?"

She grinned at my impatience. "Yes."

WHEN I ENTERED Katy's room, she was lying down, with Laura sitting beside her. I hurried over, dropped a kiss to my wife's mouth, then drew back.

"Hi, sweetheart."

She smiled up at me, clutching my hand, her eyes clouded in pain. "Hi. I'm glad you're here."

"I got here as fast as I could."

Laura grinned and stood up. "That's my cue. I'll go sit with Graham and give you two a little time alone. Come get me if you need me."

"Graham is here?"

"He didn't come with you?"

"Um, no, he didn't . . . Oh, *shit*." I shrugged my shoulders with a grimace. "I *forgot* him."

I left Graham behind in the restaurant. I ran out without telling him what happened or where I was going. Right in the middle of a pitch to a new client, as well.

Laura began to chuckle. "I left my phone in the car. I'm sure he's been calling."

I pulled out my phone from my pocket, seeing I had missed several calls and texts. I handed it to Laura. "Use mine. I owe him an apology. Or ten."

She took the phone, shaking her head. "I'm sure he'll understand." She paused beside me to give me a quick hug. "She needs you, Richard. She's scared, but trying to be brave," she whispered.

I nodded and quietly thanked her. That was my Katy. Brave and silent. My gaze followed Laura's departing form with gratitude. She was a positive force in both our lives and the closest thing to a mother I had ever truly known.

I sat beside Katy, holding her hand in mine, and looked at Suzanne.

"Well?"

"We thought maybe it was Braxton Hicks, but Katy's water broke, and her labor is progressing at a steady pace. I think you're going to meet your child today if things keep moving forward like this."

I lifted Katy's hand to my mouth, pressing a kiss on her knuckles. "Today," I repeated, meeting her anxious gaze.

"We're going to monitor Katy, and we'll move her when it's time. Meanwhile, I need you to remember everything you learned in your classes. Help her with her breathing, keep her comfortable, and let her lean on you." Her gaze went to Katy. "You can walk if you want to—in fact, I recommend it. There're ice chips and water here. Are you certain no epidural?"

Katy shook her head. She was adamant on that subject, no matter how I pleaded with her to change her mind.

Dr. Suzanne smiled at Katy and patted her hand. "You can change your mind, if you want, but we can't leave it too long. There is a point we can't go back."

"I know. I want to do this without drugs."

"Okay, you two. Settle in. I'll be back shortly."

She left, and I bent over and kissed my wife, meeting her worried gaze steadily. "I'm here, sweetheart. You're going to be fine. I won't leave you for a minute. And later, we're going to meet our child."

"It's so overwhelming," she admitted in a shaky voice. "I'm scared."

I was relieved she said the words aloud. I pressed another kiss on her head.

"What do you need?"

"You to hold me."

"You never have to ask."

She shifted to the side, and I sat beside her, wrapping my arms around her body, spreading my hand wide across her stomach, and rocking her gently until I felt her relax.

"Someone is anxious to meet you."

She hummed softly. "Meet *us*. It's your voice he or she reacts to the most."

I smiled, dropping a kiss to her hair, then stroked her swollen belly.

It had felt odd the first time I talked to her stomach. I felt like an idiot, lying beside her with my hand on her skin, muttering about silly things. Except, I liked it. I started reading books, humming music, talking about how much fun we were going to have when he or she was born—anything to connect myself to the life growing inside Katy. The first time I felt the push of a hand or foot against my skin, I actually wept. And for the second time in my life, I knew I was in love. Boy or girl, I would love and protect this child with everything in me. Knowing I would hold them in the next few hours made my chest ache with a sweetness I still wasn't used to feeling. I glanced up at Katy, who was watching me with tender eyes.

"I love you, Katy."

She smiled. "*We* love you."

She grimaced when another contraction hit, grabbing my hand.

I inhaled hard, knowing this was only the start, and hoping I was strong enough for her to lean on—both physically and emotionally. "Okay, sweetheart. Breathe with me."

Chapter 2

THINGS PROGRESSED TO the point it was time to move to the delivery room. I had walked with her until she couldn't walk anymore, fed her ice chips, rubbed her back and shoulders, and reassured her even as worry ate its way into my stomach. I blinked away tears when I saw the amount of pain she was experiencing. I let her hold my hand, not caring that she might break it with her death grip, as the contractions became stronger and closer together. She did change her mind about the epidural, and although I was grateful it took away the pain, I lost it when I saw the size of the needle they used. I had wanted to be involved, and they showed me how to hold Katy's shoulders to help with the procedure. I stepped forward to do so, caught sight of the needle, and froze. They had to push me out of the way, and the same nurse who had been at the front desk, stood in my place, all the while chuckling about "men and pain." I had a feeling I would never live it down.

I would also never live down leaving Graham behind. Apparently, after I ran out of the restaurant, he explained to our client he was certain the call I took was about my pregnant wife. He tried to chase down my car, but I didn't notice him. The client drove him back to the office, and once he spoke to Laura, he and Jenna made their way to the hospital. I gave them regular updates, and Katy and I walked down to see them. During one visit, Graham handed me my car keys and said it now was parked safely across the street. He leaned close when he muttered four hundred dollars was a bit excessive as a thank you for valet service, but I only grinned. It got me to Katy faster, and the kid probably needed it much more than I did, so I was more than okay with it. Laura came and went from the room, her quiet manner keeping us both composed. Her aura of calmness was exactly what we needed.

I bent over Katy, praising her strength and bravery. Murmuring words of encouragement. Holding her hand, stroking her forehead with cool cloths. When instructed, I moved behind her, supporting her shoulders, encouraging her to push.

When our daughter came into the world with a loud wail, I swore I had never heard a sound so beautiful. My hand was shaking as they let me cut the umbilical cord. My chest constricted, tightening to an almost painful level. My entire body vibrated as they allowed me to hold our daughter for the first time. Red-faced, wrinkled, and wet, she was the loveliest thing I'd ever seen in my life. Tufts of dark hair stuck up all around, and her eyes blinked open as she yawned, exhausted from the work of being born. For a moment, there were only the two of us in the world. I stroked her tiny cheek with my finger in wonder. Bending, I kissed Katy, who was watching us with tired, happy eyes.

"Look what we made," I whispered. "She's perfect." Carefully, I laid her back on Katy's chest, where she nuzzled contentedly. "You were incredible, sweetheart," I praised her gently. "Remarkable."

She looked down at our daughter. "We did good."

I placed one hand on our daughter's back and laid my head beside Katy's on the pillow.

"Yes, we did."

I GLANCED AT the clock, surprised how late it was. Katy was asleep, one hand curled under her cheek as she slumbered, completely exhausted. Graham, Laura, and Jenna left a few hours ago. Graham insisted I had to eat, and dragged me from the room, while Laura and Jenna stayed with Katy. I brought her back some cheese, crackers, and fruit, which she nibbled at while we all talked. Once I satisfied him, having eaten something, he took his girls home, leaving me alone with mine.

My family.

Katy tried to convince me to go home and sleep, but I didn't want to leave either of them. I couldn't. I wanted to be here with them and make sure they were both okay.

My daughter slept in my arms. She was a tiny, fragile being, who I already loved more than I thought was humanly possible. I couldn't put her down. I watched as she squirmed, swaddled in a soft, pink blanket. Her rosebud mouth was pursed, her small fists fighting to escape the material. Katy had explained the whole swaddling thing to me, but I couldn't resist loosening the cloth and letting out one of her hands. She gripped my finger with a strength that surprised and delighted me. My baby girl was strong. Her sleepy blue eyes, already so much like Katy's, peeked up at me, then drifted shut, her grip never loosening.

"She's perfect," Katy whispered.

I looked up with a grin.

"She is, Mommy."

Katy's smile was wide and beautiful. "We have to name her, Richard."

"I know. None of the ones I liked suit her now that she's here, and I can see her sweet face." I ran my finger down a plump little cheek. "Are you sure you don't want to name her after Penny?"

My wife grimaced as she pulled herself up into a sitting position. "No. She didn't like her name."

"Was there a name she did like?"

Katy pursed her lips, the expression much like our daughter's. "She liked her middle name, Grace. I like it, too," she added.

"Grace," I repeated, liking how that sounded. I looked down at my daughter. "Grace VanRyan."

"Anne is Laura's middle name," Katy offered. "Grace Anne VanRyan."

It was right. The names went well together, and they honored two women we both loved. "I love it. Laura will be thrilled, and Penny would have been so happy and proud."

Lowering my head, I kissed my baby girl. "Hello, Gracie."

"I thought you didn't like nicknames."

Standing, I slid Gracie into Katy's arms. "I thought a lot of stupid things. She looks like a Gracie." I nuzzled Katy's cheek and brushed the hair back from her face. "You, sweetheart, are supposed to be asleep."

"You should go home and get some sleep yourself."

"Nope. I paid a lot of money for this private room. I'll go home when you do."

"So stubborn."

I chuckled and took Gracie back. Katy had her long enough. "Yep. So you go to sleep. I'll just sit here with Gracie and tell her all about her crazy, adopted family and her perfect, wonderful mommy."

"What about her wonderful daddy?"

Hearing that word made me blink. Then I blinked again.

Daddy. A title I never thought would belong to me. A swell of sentiment made my throat thick. I reached out and grasped Katy's hand, needing her touch.

"I'll be the best daddy I can be."

"I know you will be. You're already the best husband."

Leaning down, I captured her mouth with mine, feeling a thousand emotions. Ones only Katy, and now Gracie, could make me feel. Feelings I didn't know existed—happiness and elation so poignant it made my chest ache. Contentment and peace that permeated my life simply from their presence. I had found a group of people I considered my family now, but Katy and Gracie belonged to *me*. They were my world, and I knew I was theirs. "Thank you, my Katy. For my daughter. For you."

She cupped my cheek. "Are you all right, Richard?"

I swallowed, turning my head, kissing her palm. I knew if I told her, she would understand. She always understood me. "It's just all . . ."

"Overwhelming? Scary?"

"Yes."

"We'll handle it together."

She was right. We handled everything together now. My wife was my rock. Still, I was worried.

I leaned closer. "I don't want to fuck her up."

She arched an eyebrow. We'd already had the "stop swearing so much" conversation—many times.

"Sorry. *Mess* her up the way my parents did me."

"You won't. I won't let you." She grinned mischievously. "Jenna and Laura would kick your ass, too."

I arched my eyebrow, pretending to cover Gracie's ears. "Now who's swearing?"

"Ass is different."

"I'll remind you of that when she shouts it out in daycare." I huffed. "Unless she's telling some boy to keep his hands to himself. Then she can use the word *ass* as much as she wants."

Katy rolled her eyes. "Let's get her eating solid food and walking before we start thinking about boys and dating, okay?"

"Good idea. Walking I can handle. She can't date until she's thirty."

"Good luck with that, Daddy."

I sat down, cooing at Gracie who was watching us, her wide, blue eyes blinking and drowsy. "You're Daddy's girl, right? No icky boys for you."

Katy muttered a mild curse, making me chuckle.

"I think Mommy is a little grumpy." I pressed a kiss to Gracie's forehead. "I think someone wore her out today."

"*You* wear me out."

"I like wearing you out."

"I'm aware—hence the baby you're holding."

I smirked, settling Gracie into the crook of my arm. She fit perfectly there. I reclined in my seat, staring at my wife. The rounder she grew while carrying Gracie, the sexier I had found her, and the more I wanted her. The new curves and the way her body responded had been like aphrodisiacs to me—not that I needed much incentive when it came to Katy. Whereas she thought she was fat, I found her sexy and alluring. I proved it to her—many times.

Katy smiled lovingly at me, her voice gentle.

"You're going to hold her all night, aren't you?"

"Probably."

"I guess it puts your theory of not loving a child to rest."

I frowned, looking down at Gracie. How I could have ever believed such a ridiculous idea now seemed so foreign to me. So wrong. I had fallen in love with her before I ever saw her on that ultrasound screen all those months ago. Then the first time I held her, I was encompassed with a love I never dreamed existed. As usual, Katy had been right.

"It was an inane theory."

"It was how you coped."

I stood, laying Gracie in her bassinet. I focused on my wife, stroking back her hair, gliding my finger down her cheek. I lifted her chin, kissing her soft lips. "That was all I did before I found you. I coped. Now I live."

She beamed up at me. "You live well."

"I do. I have a great job, a bunch of crazy friends who are like family, and the most amazing wife in the world—who today, gave me the best gift I've ever received." I kissed her again. "I'm very lucky."

"We're the lucky ones. Gracie and me. We have you."

"We have each other." I winked at her cheekily. "I think I may want a few more just like her."

Her eyes grew wide. "Um, maybe we can discuss that at a later date."

"Sure. You're young. We have time."

Katy laughed. I always teased her about being younger than I was. In truth, although chronologically I had seven years on top of her twenty-six, she was far wiser than I would ever be.

I dropped another kiss on her mouth. "Now, go to sleep. We can go home tomorrow, and I want you to get some rest."

"What about you?"

"I'll doze in the chair."

"The bed is pretty sturdy."

"Oh, yeah?"

She shifted over. "Lots of room for you and Gracie."

I paused, pursing my lips in thought. "I might get into trouble. If Shelly returns, she'll order me out. She already thinks I'm trouble."

"You *are* trouble. I doubt finding you beside me will shock her too much." Her tone changed and became serious. "I would rest better with you holding me."

That was all I needed. I scooped up Gracie and slid in beside Katy. I lifted my arm, letting her curl into my side with her head on my chest. I tucked Gracie against me and sighed in contentment. Once again, I had my family wrapped in my arms. Katy's body grew heavy with sleep and soon her even breathing let me know she was resting. Gracie snuffled and squirmed, barely waking despite all the jostling. I was certain she'd be wide-awake soon enough.

I was too wired to sleep. I lay, thinking of the past months. All the love, joy, and laughter my life now contained. All the great moments.

I looked up toward the ceiling and winked.

"You seeing this, Penny? I got your girls—just as I promised."

I knew, if she were here, she would smirk warmly at me and tell me she knew it all along. She'd say she wasn't surprised it took me longer to figure it out since Katy was the smarter of the two of us.

With a grin, I tucked my family closer.

She'd be right.

Chapter 3

GRACIE'S CRY HAD barely started, and I was out of bed. I hurried across the hall, scooping up my daughter, and cradling her to my chest.

"Hey, baby girl, it's okay. Daddy's got you."

She settled against me, her tiny fists moving restlessly on my chest as she squirmed and fussed. I knew the fussing would soon turn into cries—something I couldn't stand.

Tears never bothered me before. I could watch a woman sob and wail, and the only thing I felt was annoyed. The first time I saw Katy weep, my heart twisted with an emotion I didn't understand. Soon enough I learned I hated to see my wife cry. It did something—brought forth a protective urge I never knew I had within me. I had to fix whatever was upsetting her, although much of the time it was *me* causing the problem. Therefore, I tried not to be an ass too much of the time, although Katy liked to remind me it was deeply ingrained in my psyche.

But my daughter—Gracie crying—brought me to my knees. I couldn't bear the sounds of her shrill cries or the sight of the tears that ran down her face.

"Richard," Katy's voice broke through my musings. "You can't keep doing this."

I looked up at my wife standing in the doorway. With a smile, she handed me the bottle, and rubbed her hand down Gracie's back in long, gentle strokes. I moved to the rocker, sitting down, and getting comfortable with Gracie in the crook of my elbow. I tested the milk, then slipped the nipple into her anxious mouth. The sounds of her greedy swallows made me grin. She had a voracious appetite.

"You'd think we never fed her."

"She has your appetite. And your impatient streak." Katy stated dryly.

I chuckled. She was correct on both counts.

She sat on the footstool, gazing at me. "We agreed I'd do the night shift. You have to go back to work tomorrow. You need your sleep."

"I'm fine. She was crying."

"She barely whimpered. She might have gone back to sleep."

"I hate it when she cries," I admitted. "I'd rather get up and hold her."

"Richard—"

"I know," I grumbled. I had read the books about letting them self-soothe, and not reacting to every noise. But this was different. This was *my* daughter.

"You'll start falling asleep at your desk if you don't let me handle the nights."

"What about you?" I challenged.

"I can nap when she does. You already have someone cleaning the house, and bringing in meals. I don't have much left to do *but* nap and look after Gracie."

It took a lot of convincing, but I had insisted on making those arrangements. It was my way of caring for her.

"Good." I frowned. "I don't want to go back to work, if I'm being honest."

She tilted her head. "You don't trust me with your daughter?" she asked. Her tone was light, but I heard the worry in her voice.

I bent forward, pressing my mouth to hers. "Don't be ridiculous. Of course I do. I trust you implicitly with *our* daughter. But for the first time in my life, I don't want to go to work. I want to stay home. With the two of you." I sighed heavily. "The last two weeks have gone by far too fast."

She leaned forward, brushing my hair off my forehead. "Richard, we'll be here when you get home. And I can bring her down to see you for lunch."

"I know."

She smiled at me. My favorite of all Katy's smiles. It was *my* smile—filled with the love she showed only to me. "What's wrong, my darling? This isn't like you."

She was right. I hadn't changed that much—I was still the practical, no-nonsense one. I approached everything with the same can-do attitude. Everything, that was, except my family. It was entirely different. I met Katy's concerned stare and inhaled deeply. I knew I could tell her what I was feeling and she would understand.

She always understood.

"She changes every day. I feel like I'm going to miss something," I confessed. "I won't be here to hear her first words or watch her first steps." I sighed trying to explain. "I feel as if I've been given a gift and I don't want to squander it. I suppose that sounds crazy, weak even, but it's how I feel."

"It doesn't sound crazy or weak. It sounds like a father who loves his child." She studied me. "You never give yourself enough credit. You've come so far, Richard. I'm very proud of you."

I ducked my head at her praise. I had changed—I knew that. I was still changing. Having Gracie now brought out a whole new level of emotions, and I was having a hard time acclimating myself to them.

"This is new to both of us, you know," she added. "I worry, too."

"You seem so calm all the time."

She shook her head. "I must hide it well. I'm a mess, constantly second-guessing myself and every decision I make."

Her words surprised me. "I think you're amazing."

"I feel the same way about you."

"We're a good team." I mused. "Even if we're both a hot mess."

"We'll figure it out together. And we'll miss you, but you need to go back to work."

"I could quit. I don't *have* to work."

She chuckled. "And in about a month, you would be going crazy, no matter how much you love Gracie. You would miss it too much and be begging Graham to take you back."

She was right. She was always right.

Katy rubbed my hand that was holding Gracie. "Richard, she's three weeks old. She won't be walking or talking for a while. And you could work from your office here, and she might still say Dada for the first time while you're out of the room."

I interrupted her. "You think she'll say Dada first?"

She laughed with a shake of her head. "I have no doubt you'll do everything you can to make sure of it."

I sighed. "You're right. I know you're right. It's probably just . . . hormones talking."

Her eyes widened. "Um, hormones? I think that's my department."

"Sympathy ones." I lifted one shoulder. "There's been a lot of them around the place lately."

She chuckled. "I'll give you that. You're surrounded by estrogen now." She leaned closer, kissing me. "I promise, I'll send you videos and pictures every day. And if I think she's going to talk, I'll video it for you."

"When her butt starts to wiggle . . ."

"Yep. On it. Maybe once she starts crawling, we can have Jenna do a walking countdown. She can build one of her infamous charts. You can work from home."

I narrowed my eyes. "Are you making fun of me?"

"No. Never."

I pulled the bottle away, and lifted Gracie to my shoulder, patting her back. "I think you are."

"Maybe a little." She kissed me. "But I love you so much because you want to be here." She met my eyes. "Quite a change from the Richard I first met."

I snorted. "He was an ass."

She quirked her eyebrow.

I pouted, hoping for another kiss, which I got. Gracie chose that moment to let out a loud belch and promptly filled her diaper.

Holy fuck. For something so cute, she could still make me gag on occasion. This was one of them.

The stench was horrendous.

I stood, holding my breath. "You're right. I need to sleep." I dropped a fast kiss to Gracie's cheek and handed her off to Katy. "All yours."

I hurried away, my eyes smarting from not breathing. But I could still smell it.

Katy laughed behind me. "Daddy's still an ass," she crooned to Gracie.

"I know," I called. I was okay with that. At least I could breathe.

Katy

I WOKE UP, hearing soft whispers. I rolled over, guessing correctly that Richard had once again gotten out of bed and was in the nursery. His side of the bed was vacant, and the monitor lit up as he spoke to our daughter while feeding her. I loved hearing him chat to her. Richard never minced words—not even with me. He was a straight shooter and spoke his mind. He showed me a gentler side when we fell in love, but his personality never changed much. He was still demanding and blunt. He had learned, however, to rein in the harsher side of his character, and knew how to deal with people now. At least most of the time.

But with Gracie he was different.

With her, he was soft. That was the only way to describe it. He changed completely with her. She brought forth the tender, loving man in him. He hurried home at night, anxious to be with us. He reached for her as soon as he came in the door, ready to forget businessman Richard, and assume the role of Daddy. He laughed and made funny faces, he read her books, and did voices to make her gurgle and smile. He told her amusing stories of his clients, using a singsong voice, even when he cursed. I had admonished him over it, but he simply looked at me, flummoxed.

"The book, Katy," he insisted. "The book said at this early stage she doesn't understand the words, it's the tone. Fuck is just like blanket to her. All of it is gibberish. I keep my tone light, and it makes her happy."

"If her first word is a curse, you're explaining that to Graham."

"Pretty sure Graham won't be shocked."

"Laura might box your ears."

"I'd like to see her try."

"Richard—"

"I'll tone it down." He turned his head, cooing at Gracie who stared up at him from his broad shoulder, her blue eyes fixed on his face. "Mommy is such a worrywart."

She flapped her little gums, and I held back my grin, knowing what would happen next. She opened her mouth and spewed on him, the splatter dripping down his expensive dress shirt. Once again he had neglected to use a towel.

I had to walk away I was laughing so hard. He never learned.

But right now, there were no curse words. There was Richard, murmuring low to Gracie. I had given up fighting him about nights. In the weeks since he'd returned to work, I realized this was *their* time. He'd talk and croon to her. I swore I heard him giggle. And he'd sing.

He had the worst singing voice I had ever heard. It was off key and sounded like someone dying in the bathtub. He only ever sang when they were alone. I made the mistake of giggling once when he tried to warble the song from *Frozen*, thinking she'd like it. I gaped for a minute at the odd noise coming from his throat. I was so used to him being good at everything, that finding something he wasn't perfect at caught me off guard. He glared, huffed, and strode out of the room with her, leaving me snorting on the sofa. After that, he refused to sing in front of me.

I loved to hear him anyway, and so did Gracie. There was no doubt she was Daddy's girl, and he soothed her better than anyone—including me.

She was fussier than normal tonight. And I was restless. I sat up, pushing my hair back from my head, listening to them.

"Hey, baby girl, what's going on?" he murmured. "You need something? Tell Daddy and he'll do it."

Gracie gurgled and kept fussing. There was some movement, and then the soft strains of music. Richard began to hum, the sound low, and nowhere near as bad as his singing. Gracie snuffled loudly and began to quiet down. I slipped out of bed and padded across the hall, stopping in the doorway. My chest tightened at the sight before me.

Richard, tall, broad, and bare chested, cradling his daughter close, and dancing with her. She was tucked high on his chest, with his cheek resting on her head. Her tiny hand was encased inside his, and he held her protectively. No doubt his humming was soothing to her, rumbling through his chest and lulling her into peace.

Tears filled my eyes watching them. The cold-hearted man I first knew was gone and replaced by this protector who would do anything to care for his child. To care for me.

I sniffled and began to back out to leave them, when his head lifted. He met my eyes, and held out his hand, beckoning me to them. I crossed the room. He drew me close, still moving, and pressed a kiss to my head. He wrapped his arm around me, and we moved, a small family wrapped together in the dark.

"You're supposed to be sleeping," he murmured.

"I heard you and came to see what you were doing."

"She likes it when we dance."

"You never told me that."

He shrugged in the dim light. "It's sort of our thing when she's really fussy."

I stroked down her back, smiling at my daughter. She was out now, her cheek pressed to his chest, with her tiny rosebud mouth open. Her long lashes fluttered on her cheek.

"I think it worked."

"It usually does."

I tilted my head. "She's a lucky girl having you as her daddy."

He smiled down at me, his hazel eyes glittering in the low light. "I'm the lucky one."

Our gazes locked and held. The air around us grew heavier. Richard's arm tightened around me. "Katy," he breathed.

"I saw Suzanne last week."

"And?"

"We're all clear."

"Why didn't you say anything?"

I inhaled. "I wasn't ready."

"But you are now?"

I stretched up, pressing my lips to his. He had grown a beard while he was at home, and I liked it so much, he kept it when he returned to work. He kept it short and trimmed, but I loved how it felt against my skin as his mouth moved with mine. Our kiss was long, deep, and slow. He groaned low in his chest, then dropped another kiss to my mouth. "Sweetheart?"

I stepped back, knowing now why I was so restless, and exactly how to ease it. I needed Richard.

"This girl needs something, too."

"Tell me," he demanded quietly.

"I need *you*. Put Gracie down, and come back to bed."

He quirked his eyebrow, grinning widely. He tenderly laid her down, making sure she was content. He ran his hand down her back, his fingers spread wide, staying in place for a moment.

Then he turned to me, and I caught my breath. His sleep pants hung low on his hips, his erection pressing against the material. He stalked across the nursery, reaching out, dragging me to his chest and kissing me hard.

"Are you sure?"

I wrapped my arms around his neck. "Yes."

He swept me up in his arms, his mouth covering mine. "Thank God."

Our lips never separated. He set me on my feet by our bed, impatiently tugging my nightgown over my head. As the air hit my bare skin, I shivered and crossed my arms over my chest, suddenly feeling shy.

Richard stopped with a frown. "What? What's wrong?"

"I–I've changed a little." I had stretch marks, and my stomach wasn't as flat as it used to be. Richard was still lean and hard, his body perfection in my eyes.

He smiled, stepping close, and loosening my arms. "Yes, you have. You've gotten even more beautiful." He ran his finger over my hips, feathering the small stripes along the side. "These are just marks, Katy. They're part of you, and I love them because of how they got there. You carried my child—our child—and they're sexy because of that."

He slid his hands up my body, cupping my breasts. They were fuller now and more sensitive than ever. I moaned as he stroked my nipples. "I've missed these. I've missed you." He nudged me onto the bed, hovering over me. "I've missed being with you."

"So have I." A low gasp escaped my throat as he dragged his mouth across my skin. The feel of his rough scruff on my body was different and amazing.

"Like that?" he asked, rubbing his chin along my stomach. "You like how that feels, sweetheart?"

"Yes."

He lowered his head. "Then you're really gonna like this."

Richard

FUCK, IT HAD been so long since we were like this. Together, naked, and ready for each other. I hadn't wanted to push her and tried to be patient, even though patience wasn't my strongest trait. The fact she came to me was a huge turn on, and seeing her need, I planned to meet and exceed her desire. She was softer, curvier than before she got pregnant, and I loved how she felt under my hands.

Her low hiss when I buried my face between her legs made me smile against her slick skin. She was so ready for me. I was so fucking ready. Everything about her was as new as it was familiar: her sounds, her taste, the way she moved against my mouth. I teased and licked, groaning at her reactions, making a mental note to keep the beard. Jenna teased me mercilessly at work, but it was worth this effect on my wife. She came hard and fast, her cries low and needy. I sat up with a grin, and settled between her legs. The blunt head of my cock nudged at her entrance, the heat beckoning and welcome.

"My turn, baby."

Her incredible eyes glittered in the dimness. "Richard . . . *yes* . . ."

I slid inside her slowly, her pussy tight and wet around me. Once I was buried deep within her, I stilled, our gazes locking as I began to move, long, even thrusts that made us both groan. "So much better than my hand," I teased, reminding her of our early days.

Katy tightened her grip on my shoulders. "Harder," she pleaded. "Fuck me, Richard. Just *fuck* me."

Jesus.

She rarely swore, and hearing that sweet mouth of hers utter dirty words cranked me even higher. I pushed at her knees, opening her up even more, sinking deeper. The weight of my body pressed her into the mattress, and I let go, slamming into her with hard, powerful strokes. We moved together, and I kissed and licked at her body, nibbled at her collarbones, and skimmed my tongue up her neck, swirling it on the sensitive skin behind her ear. Our mouths fused together, exploring each other, and her taste wrecked me. I nipped at her full lips, easing the sting with soft presses of my mouth. Our skin slid together, the dampness warm and making the friction even more profound. My orgasm began to build, my balls tightening.

"*Oh God*—Katy . . ."

She cried out, flexing around me, and I buried my face in her neck as I spilled inside, breathing out her name, then collapsing beside her, wrapping her in my arms.

For a few moments, there was only the sound of our fast breathing. Then she spoke.

"You're keeping the beard."

I chuckled. "Done."

Katy curled into me, running her fingers through my hair. I huffed a long breath—I loved it when she did that. I felt myself relaxing into her warmth and sliding into sleep.

I had a feeling I'd be getting even less rest than usual for the next while. Both my girls needed attention now.

And I was good with that.

Chapter 4

Richard

I WRAPPED A towel around Gracie and tucked her against my chest. She grizzled and grasped against my skin, her legs bending and stretching. She was anxious to get going. At six months old, from the second she opened her eyes, until they finally, *begrudgingly*, shut for the night, she was on the go. There was a lot of bum wiggling these days—I had many videos on my phone from Katy, and I had witnessed it many times, but she hadn't yet started crawling, although I expected it any day.

I had taken her in the shower with me. She loved showers and I didn't want to leave her alone too long. She laughed the whole time, and though I couldn't say I was as clean as I normally would be, I would pass for the day.

I carefully patted her hair dry after I fastened her diaper. The sounds of Katy being ill made me hurry back to our room. Last night, she had suddenly wanted Japanese food. She disliked sushi but loved tempura. When she called and asked me to bring home dinner, I was only too happy to pick up a huge assortment of sushi for me, and tempura for her from my favorite place. I chuckled as she nibbled on a few Ebi and California rolls—the only kind of sushi she would eat. She ignored my teasing that it wasn't really sushi since the shrimp was cooked and the other was just vegetables. She ate heartily, but began to feel ill a couple hours after dinner, and had been up most of the night. I blamed the Ebi.

Bad shrimp was hell.

Between her retching, and the contents of Gracie's diaper this morning, I was feeling a little under the weather myself. Whoever said this shit, pardon the pun, got easier, was a fucking liar. Katy seemed to handle it all fine, but I still gagged on occasion. How something so small and adorable could produce nuclear explosions the way Gracie did was a mystery.

I knocked on the bathroom door. "Okay, sweetheart?"

A few second later, Katy shuffled out, looking like hell. She was pale and shaky, her hair a plastered mess on one side of her head.

"No," she replied shortly, falling back on the bed.

I pulled up the covers. "Mrs. Brandon is going to check on you this morning while she's cleaning."

"You can't be serious about taking Gracie into work with you," she protested.

"You can't look after her. Laura is away. The only other person we trust is down with the flu, so I doubt two nauseous women will help Gracie much. I have her playpen and toys in the office. I'll lay her down for a nap before I head to the meeting, and once it's done, I'll come home and look after you."

"What if she won't nap?"

"Stop worrying. Jenna and Amy are there. All the women in the office love her. Graham is as good with her as I am. She'll be fine." I was telling the truth. She was a familiar visitor to the office, and they all loved spoiling her. Graham doted on her, and he was one of her favorite people.

"She's been acting strange with people. And she's teething."

I laid Gracie beside Katy and ran my hand through her hair. Gracie kicked her legs, cooing at her mother. "I have this covered. Just let me run and get dressed, and brush my teeth. Make sure she doesn't roll off the bed."

She looped an arm around Gracie. "Got her."

I rushed to the closet, throwing on my pants. I brushed my teeth and grabbed my shirt. Back in our room, Gracie was busy gnawing on her toes as she lay in the circle of Katy's arms. I scooped her up and tucked the blanket around Katy. "I'll be back once she's fed."

"Mm'kay," she mumbled, already drifting.

She slept the whole time I was gone, which I hope meant she was done being ill. I fed Gracie, burped and got her dressed, then managed to finish getting myself ready after tucking her into my sock drawer for safe keeping, as I pulled on my suit. I sang to her, as I yanked on my socks and did my tie. Katy laughed when I sang, but Gracie loved it. She could appreciate my unique tone. I think it soothed her. Or at the very least, it confused her so much, she forgot to be upset. Either way worked.

Finally, I checked her bag, grateful Katy was so organized, and it was already packed, then strapped her into the front facing carrier on my chest. She loved it. Her hands flapped, and her feet kicked every time she was in it. I grabbed my briefcase and went back to our room.

"We're off, Mommy."

Katy opened one eye. I grinned at her and struck a pose. "On a scale of one to ten, how incredibly sexy am I carrying the cutest baby in the world? Pretty irresistible, right?"

Katy slapped a hand over her mouth and tore past me to the bathroom. I grimaced at the sound of more retching. I guess she wasn't done.

"I'm going to assume Mommy thinks we're a ten. Who could resist us?" I looked down at Gracie who frowned up at me, drool running down her chin as she gummed her fingers. Oh God, I hoped she wasn't going to be cranky, or this could be one long ass day.

She gurgled her agreement, as I glanced at the bathroom door, worried about Katy. It was so unusual for her to be ill, I wasn't sure what to do to help. I tapped on the door, waiting for her to respond. She hated it when I hovered.

She came out, and I helped her into bed. Gracie waved her arms in excitement at seeing Katy.

"Maybe I should stay home."

"Go, Richard," she insisted. "I'll be fine."

"Are you sure?" I really hated leaving her, even though it was important. We had worked long and hard on this campaign and the meeting with the client was today. The client was a bit of a hard-ass and Graham insisted I be the one to handle it, and I didn't want to let him down, but Katy was more important.

"Yes. All I'm going to do is sleep. Go!"

I ran a hand through my hair. "Call me if you need me. I'll come home right away."

"I will."

"I'll be home as soon as the meeting is done."

"Okay." She groaned as she rolled over and shut her eyes. "I'll be here."

I hurried to the car and strapped Gracie into her car seat. Just in case, I slipped her a soother. Katy hated them, but today, I needed all the help I could get.

GRACIE FUSSED MOST of the morning, only settling when I was close. I gave up and strapped her into the carrier, and let her play with my fingers as I went through all the last minute details for the meeting. Jenna was racing around, making sure the boardroom was set up, and Amy stayed close, helping me with any final items and adjustments. Forty-five minutes before the meeting, I sat down and fed Gracie. Her eyelids began to droop and I had to hold back from punching the air in victory. If she followed her normal schedule, I'd burp her, she'd drink a little more, and then be out for the next of couple hours. I'd be done with the meeting, Graham would take the client to lunch, and I could go home and make sure Katy was okay. I was distracted as I lifted her to my shoulder, forgetting the towel until I felt the wetness of her regurgitation soak through my shirt. I shut my eyes and groaned. I had dropped a bunch of shirts at the dry cleaners yesterday and hadn't brought a fresh one in with me. Hopefully, I would have a few minutes to try and rinse it. I huffed out a long breath, and cradled Gracie in my arms, slipping the nipple into her mouth.

"Let's try and help Daddy out, okay? No more spewing or diaper filling until after the meeting. How about that?"

She gurgled up at me, her fat cheeks pink from teething. I had rubbed her gums with the stuff Katy used, so I hoped it would help. She pulled on her bottle, and slowly her eyes began to drift back shut. Jenna came in, and I lifted my head, eyes wide to warn her to be quiet. She grinned at me and whispered as she came closer.

"I got Samantha coming to work in here while we're in the meeting. She'll come get you if needed."

I frowned. "Can't Amy do it?" Gracie knew Amy, at least, if she woke up. I didn't want her frightened.

"She has all your files, and you need her."

She was right, but still, I worried.

"We're right down the hall."

I stood and carried Gracie to her playpen, settling her inside, and draping a blanket over her.

"Okay."

"Are you, ah, gonna change your shirt?"

I glanced at my shoulder with a grimace. "I don't have another one. I'll go rinse it out. I'll meet you there in ten minutes."

"He's already here."

I sucked in a breath, trying to be patient. I was reaching my limit for the day. "Five, then." I'd have to forgo trying to dry it.

"Okay."

I PAUSED IN my presentation to take a sip of water. So far, things were going well. Mr. Cunningham had been onboard with most of the campaign, asking for clarification or wanting small changes. Graham had been jotting down notes, and Amy made some for me. He was a tough nut to crack, never smiling or seemingly overly impressed, but at least he hadn't disliked what I had done. He had been the same in all our preliminary meetings, so I was prepared for his stoic reaction.

As we moved to the next part of the campaign, I saw Jenna glance down at her phone, then at me. She averted her eyes, offered a quiet apology, and slipped out of the boardroom, pushing the door shut behind her. But that was all it took.

The boardroom at the Gavin Group was soundproofed, so you weren't disturbed during a meeting. But when the door opened, I heard it. The wailing of a child in the building.

My child.

I met Graham's eyes. He had heard her, as well. His gaze was calm, and I glanced down at my notes, faltering for a moment. A rare occurrence for me.

Obviously, Jenna had gone to help Samantha out. She would sooth Gracie, and I would be done here in about thirty minutes, and I would take over. I knew I had to finish this. She'd be fine, I assured myself. Business came first. I cleared my throat. "As I was saying," I began.

Except I swore I could hear her, even with the door closed. The piercing cry I hated the most—the one that spoke of desperate need. It didn't happen very often, but when it did, I couldn't ignore it. Not when I was at home, and most certainly not now.

"I apologize, Mr. Cunningham. I need five minutes," I blurted, setting down the papers. "Please have a coffee or stretch your legs, I'll be right back."

I was out of the boardroom like a shot, not even looking to see what reaction my abrupt departure caused. In the hallway, Gracie's cries were even more heartbreaking, and I rushed to my office. Jenna was holding her, attempting to calm my screaming child, but her face told me I had made the right decision. I reached for Gracie at the same time her chubby arms stretched toward me. I gathered her close, murmuring low words of comfort. She, in turn, heaved a long stuttering breath, then upchucked all over my suit.

"*Fuck!*"

I met Jenna's amused gaze.

"Better you than me." She wrinkled her nose and took a step back. "I don't suppose you have a clean suit here, either."

I shook my head. "I'll figure something out. Your father is gonna be pissed about this. Cover for me. I'll be back as soon as possible."

She grinned. "He'll be fine. I'm sure he can tell you stories from my childhood. I remember visiting once and throwing up on his desk while he was on a conference call. He started gagging, and my mother had to drag me out, screaming. I recall her trying not to laugh."

I chuckled. "Thanks for sharing."

She winked, then left with a wave.

I carried Gracie into my bathroom, shrugged off my jacket, and laid it on the counter for her. It was ruined anyway. I stripped her down, wiping her body off with a warm cloth. I changed her diaper, and tugged a fresh onesie on her, the whole time talking to her in a quiet voice. I cheated and slipped in the soother again after rubbing more gel on her gums. Her big eyes followed my every movement, but at least she'd stopped crying. I glanced in the mirror with a small grimace. You could see the stain on my shoulder, but luckily, the suit jacket had protected my tie. I had no choice but to go back into the meeting without it.

Samantha was waiting when I returned, a bottle ready, but as soon as I tried to hand Gracie off, she began to cry and kick her legs.

"She'll be fine once I start feeding her. They're waiting for you," she assured me, taking Gracie from my arms.

I swallowed my retort, and turned to leave. I only made it to the door when the sobs got to me. Turning, I looked at my daughter. Her cheeks were wet with tears as she fought against Samantha. Her pathetic expression was fucking killing me, and then she said it.

"Dada," she whimpered out. I was certain I heard it, although Samantha didn't react. But it was clear—she didn't want her damn bottle. She wanted me.

There was no choice to be made.

"Fuck it," I muttered.

I WAS SURE Graham's eyebrows hit his hairline when I walked back into the boardroom, complete with Gracie strapped to my chest, a soother stuffed in her mouth, and a bottle ready in case. Jenna glanced away, trying not to laugh.

Mr. Cunningham looked shocked.

"I apologize. My wife is ill at home, and my daughter won't settle for anyone but me. I know this seems unorthodox, but let me finish."

I sighed in relief when he nodded. I would take whatever shit Graham gave me later, but right now, I had to make sure Gracie was okay, and please the client.

I could do both.

Forty minutes later, Gracie was asleep, my voice and the constant movement as I paced the boardroom pacifying her. Mr. Cunningham shook my hand, and for the first time ever, smiled. "Brilliant," he praised.

"Thank you. Sorry about the interruption."

He shook his head. "Do you know how often I had to stop meetings or be interrupted when my children were small? My wife worked with me, and we had an office for the kids, but invariably they would find me when they wanted something. I wouldn't change those memories for anything." He eyed me for a moment, his gaze thoughtful. "I want to do business where family is first, and the people share my values. You proved to me it is here. The contract is yours."

I didn't know how to respond—those were words I never thought anyone would ever utter to me.

Graham chuckled. "Looks like Gracie was our ringer, Richard."

Bending my head, I pressed a kiss to her fuzzy curls. She woke up as soon as I stopped walking, but was happy as long as she was close.

"I guess she is."

Mr. Cunningham laughed, and patted Gracie's head. She grabbed at his fingers, pulling on them and making him laugh. "I hope to see more of her." He turned to Graham. "Shall we discuss the logistics?"

Graham extended his arm. "Jenna, show Mr. Cunningham to my office." Then he turned to me. "Go home. You look a fright, and I'm sure your wife needs you." He leaned forward, trying to hide his amusement. "A piece of fatherly advice. You should always look down, Richard."

I glanced down at my feet and cringed. I hadn't noticed the splatter on my shoe.

I had to join in his laughter. He was right. In addition to my shoe, my suit was ruined, my shoulder a mess, and Gracie, before falling asleep, had drooled all over my hand and arm, so the sleeve was soaked. I knew my hair was sticking up everywhere from my anxious tugging, and the front of me felt far too damp and warm. I had a feeling I didn't have the diaper on as snugly as I should. I needed to go home, get cleaned up, and look after my wife.

I shook his hand. "Will do."

He shook his head as he left the boardroom. "It's never dull with you, Richard. Ever."

Laughing, I made my way to my office, and gathered up all the baby things scattered around. It surprised me still how many items it took to keep a human this small alive and happy while you were out of the house.

Still, I wouldn't change a thing.

I SETTLED INTO the chair on the deck with a relieved groan. Gracie was asleep, I was clean, and Katy was resting. I had tried repeatedly to get Gracie to say "Dada" again so Katy could hear it, but she chose to remain silent.

"Honestly, Katy. She *said* it."

She patted my cheek. "I believe you."

I knew without a doubt, she was lying. But Gracie had said it while she was reaching for me. Or it may have been duh, but I was certain it was Dada.

The house was quiet, the sun beginning to set, and I was enjoying a hard-earned beer and sandwich. The water in the pool shimmered in the evening light, and I decided I'd have a dip once I finished eating.

I had spoken to Graham, and he told me the contract had been signed. I laughed at his description of me striding back into the boardroom with Gracie strapped to my chest, and a bottle in my hand, determined to finish my presentation. "Not a sight I ever thought I'd see when it came to you, Richard. I almost fell off my chair."

I had to agree with him. It wasn't something I ever saw happening, either. Only a couple years ago, if I had been at a meeting and witnessed what occurred today, I would have rolled my eyes, thought the man was an idiot, and would never have done business with the company.

How I had changed.

Graham was glad to hear Katy felt better and Gracie had settled. We were both shocked about the fact it was my attention to my child that swung things in my favor. We never would have guessed under that unsmiling countenance beat the heart of a devoted family man.

"Like you," he added with a laugh.

And he was right. When it came to my family, Graham was right.

"I think Gracie can sit out the Conrad presentation next week. We don't want to get in trouble with the labor laws or anything," he teased.

"We'll only keep her for the real tough cases."

"Right," I snickered and hung up.

I drained my beer, headed to the cottage, and changed into my trunks. I set the baby monitor beside the pool, and dove in, the cool water refreshing. I swam some laps, surprised to find Katy sitting on the edge of the pool when I reach the end.

"Hey, sweetheart." I pushed up out of the water and kissed her. "You look better."

"I feel better."

"Good."

"Gracie is sleeping hard."

I smirked. "She had a big day. It's not every day a baby is the deciding factor in a business deal, you know."

She chuckled, the sound echoing in the quiet of the evening.

"Did you eat?"

She shook her head. "I had some ginger ale. I'll try something later."

"No more Ebi, I guess," I teased, rubbing her legs.

"Not for a while."

"I'm sorry—the one time you want Japanese food, it makes you sick."

She studied me for a moment, then bent low, meeting my gaze steadily. "It wasn't the sushi."

"It wasn't?"

"Think about it, my darling. You weren't ill."

"True. I thought it was the Ebi. I only had a couple."

She chuckled. "A couple? The way you inhaled it, I don't think so."

"What was it then? The flu?" I groaned. "God, I hope I don't get it. Or even worse, Gracie." The thought of her sick made me shudder. Lord only knew what smells she'd produce then.

"Not the flu. The baby."

I frowned in confusion. "Gracie made you sick?"

"Not *that* baby."

"Do you have a fever, Katy? You're not making any sense. We only have one baby."

"For now."

It took a moment to sink in. When the words did, I stared at her, then at her stomach. *"Again?"* I gasped. "I bought condoms!"

"And how often have we used them?"

I was at a loss for an answer. I did get carried away fast when it came to my wife. I remember opening the box—I think.

"I did it again? Knocked you up?"

"Either you or the pool boy."

I narrowed my eyes. "We don't *have* a pool boy."

"Then it's on you. Gracie is going to have a baby brother or sister in about seven months." She grinned. "Dr. Suzanne called you an overachiever."

Holy shit.

I wrapped my hands around her calves, staring at her legs. She let me process. She always knew what I needed. My mind raced—I hadn't expected this. Gracie was only six months old. We'd have two children under the age of two. Our busy lives would get even busier. Then I thought of the love I had for Gracie. The way it felt when I held her in my arms. The way it made me feel when it was my touch or voice that she needed. How *big* it made me feel. It was everything. She and Katy were the most important things in my life. I lifted my gaze to meet my wife's watchful scrutiny. Her expression was joyful, and her eyes danced. She was thrilled.

Then I realized, so was I.

With a whoop, I pulled her into the water, snickering at her gasp. I covered her mouth with mine, holding her tight with one hand, and gripping the side of the pool with the other. I kissed her hard, long, and deep.

Pulling back, I rested my forehead on hers. "So, today was morning sickness?"

She had struggled with that when she was pregnant with Gracie.

"Yes."

"Morning sickness is a crap name for it, by the way. They need to improve their marketing. Anytime projectile vomit is more accurate."

She laughed in agreement.

"And the Japanese food was a craving?"

"Yes. I had suspected yesterday, and Suzanne confirmed it this morning when she called with the news." She smiled. "I didn't want to tell you while I was throwing up and all. Give you the wrong idea that maybe I wasn't happy."

"But you are?"

"Yes."

"So am I." I pulled her closer. "Another baby. Good thing we bought a big house."

"Good thing I love you so much I don't mind being knocked up again."

I dropped a kiss to her head. "Good thing, indeed. Think it will be a boy this time?"

"We'll find out soon enough."

I eased us into the shallow end, and held her close. "Yep. And if not, we can keep trying."

"Is that a fact?"

"I'm willing to give it my best shot. Show Suzanne how much of an overachiever I really am."

She sighed in contentment. "This from the man who didn't want children."

"I want everything with you." I squeezed her, suddenly feeling serious. I spread my hand over her stomach. "Thank you, my Katy."

"I love you, Richard."

"I love you, sweetheart." I smiled. "I love you, and I love our life." I knew how lucky I was. How different my life had become, how I had changed since I fell in love with her. She had changed me for the better. She filled my life with great moments. The ones Penny told me to hold on to.

She covered my hand with hers, looking up at me.

"Me, too."

I bent down and kissed her. The monitor crackled and Gracie's babble filled the air.

"Dadadadadada."

I fist pumped the air. "Told you!"

She laughed. "I guess you did. You're being paged."

I hauled myself out of the pool, grabbed a towel, and headed toward the house and my new, favorite sound.

Dada.

Yeah. Another great moment.

Thanks to my family, life was full of them.

Acknowledgements

MANY THANKS TO my lovely group of prereaders. Karen, Janett, Beth, Darlene, Shelly, and Lisa. I appreciate all you do and all your support.

Thank you to Suzanne, Deb, Trina, and Pam. You are amazing.

Karen—your friendship—words cannot express it properly. Not even mine.

Jeanne—many thanks for your work, my friend. You mean more than you know.

To all the bloggers who devote so much time to us authors, and our words, thank you is not enough.

Thank you to my reading group—Melanie's Minions. You make it fun!

Matt—I love you. Always. There is nothing else as important.

Other Books by

MELANIE MORELAND

Into the Storm
Beneath the Scars
Over the Fence
The Contract
It Started with a Kiss

Coming in September 2017 from Random House, Loveswept
My Image of You

About the Author

NEW YORK TIMES/USA Today bestselling author Melanie Moreland, lives a happy and content life in a quiet area of Ontario with her beloved husband of twenty-seven-plus years and their rescue cat Amber. Nothing means more to her than her friends and family, and she cherishes every moment spent with them.

While seriously addicted to coffee, and highly challenged with all things computer-related and technical, she relishes baking, cooking, and trying new recipes for people to sample. She loves to throw dinner parties, and enjoys travelling, here and abroad, but finds coming home is always the best part of any trip.

Melanie delights in a good romance story with some bumps along the way, but is a true believer in happily ever after. When her head isn't buried in a book, it is bent over a keyboard, furiously typing away as her characters dictate their creative storylines to her, often with a large glass of wine keeping her company.

Connect with the author
@MorelandMelanie
www.facebook.com/authormoreland

18157325R00027

Printed in Poland
by Amazon Fulfillment
Poland Sp. z o.o., Wrocław